Once Upon a Time

For Jasmine

Second U.S. paperback edition 1998

ISBN 0-7636-0530-1

4 6 8 10 9 7 5 3

Printed in Hong Kong

Candlewick Press
2067 Massachusetts Avenue
Cambridge, Massachusetts 02140

Once Upon a Time

conceived and illustrated by
John Prater

text by
Vivian French

DISCOVERY TOYS   CANDLEWICK PRESS

Early in the morning,
Cat and me.

Not much to do.
Not much to see.

Dad's off to work now,
Mom's up too.

Not much to see.
Not much to do.

Day's getting older,
Sun's up high.

Wave to a little girl
Hurrying by.

Mom's cleaning windows.
There's a bear.

He's making a fuss
About a chair.

Ride my tricycle
For a while.

There's an egg
With a happy smile.

Mom's in the garden,
Laundry's dry.

Why do babies
Always cry?

We've got sandwiches—
Cheese today.

Why's that wolf saying,
"Come this way"?

I like jumping
To and fro.

That wolf's howling.
He's hurt his toe.

Mom's drinking coffee
By the door.

I can jump
That far and more!

Sun's going down now
In the sky.

Here's Dad home again!
We say, "Hi!"

Dad's washing dishes.
I look out.

Did I hear someone
Prowling about?

Time for my story.
I yawn and say,

"Nothing much happened
Around here today."

Read it again

Many well-known stories and rhymes feature in the text and illustrations of this book. You may enjoy looking back through the pictures to tell the tale of each set of characters. You could also find and read the original versions of these stories and rhymes.

The Family
What happens to the little boy's cat?

The Three Little Pigs
Who wants to blow their house in?

Goldilocks and the Three Bears
Who fixes the broken chair?

The Witch
Why does she
get angry?

The Giant
Whose tail does
he step on?

**Hey Diddle,
Diddle**
Can you sing
the song about the
cat and the fiddle?

Humpty Dumpty
Can you say a rhyme
about him?

**Little Red Riding
Hood**
What
happens
to her?

Reading and Writing

If you and your child have enjoyed reading this book together, you may also enjoy writing about it together. Shared writing, like shared reading, is a wonderful way to help develop children's early literacy skills. Encourage children to write or draw their own version of the story, their feelings toward the story, or an experience from their life that relates to the story in some way. You may wish to paste their work on these two pages as a keepsake and a record of their literacy development. Children not yet ready to write may enjoy dictating a story for you to write down for them. For more information and ideas about writing and reading with your child, please see the *Reading Together at Home Parents' Handbook.*

Reading Together at Home

Blue Level: Next Steps

How this book helps support your child's reading development:

Once Upon a Time imaginatively joins large colorful illustrations
with simple verses to create a hilarious story that beginning readers
can follow on their own. In this Next Steps story, a child describes
an ordinary day, but the pictures tell of an extraordinary day
occurring all around him. Children will enjoy using their knowledge
of familiar nursery stories to recognize characters in the illustrations.
They can use the pictures to retell this story and a host of others.
Doing so will help them to feel more confident and successful as readers.

See the *Reading Together at Home Parents' Handbook* for
more information on specific reading skills your child is developing
as he or she reads books in the Next Steps level
of the *Reading Together at Home* series.